THIS LITTLE TIGER BOOK BELONGS TO:

_____

_____

_____

_____

For William and Timothy
– J.S.

For Nina, with love
– T.W.

LITTLE TIGER PRESS
An imprint of Magi Publications
1 The Coda Centre, 189 Munster Road,
London SW6 6AW
First published in Great Britain 1996
This paperback edition published 1996
Text © 1996 Julie Sykes
Illustrations © 1996 Tim Warnes
Julie Sykes and Tim Warnes have asserted their rights
to be identified as the author and illustrator of this work
under the Copyright, Designs and Patents Act, 1988.
Printed in Belgium by Proost NV, Turnhout
All rights reserved
ISBN 1 85430 401 1
12 14 16 18 20 19 17 15 13 11

Shhh!

by Julie Sykes

illustrated by Tim Warnes

LITTLE TIGER PRESS

London

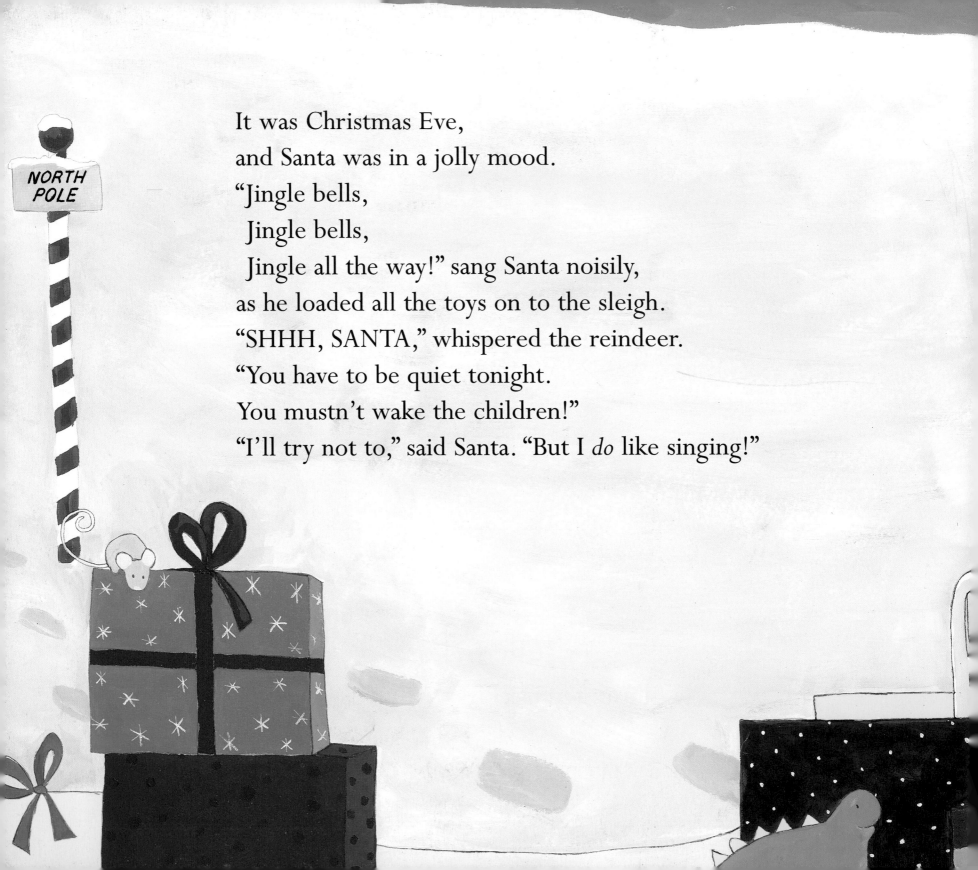

It was Christmas Eve,

and Santa was in a jolly mood.

"Jingle bells,

 Jingle bells,

 Jingle all the way!" sang Santa noisily,

as he loaded all the toys on to the sleigh.

"SHHH, SANTA," whispered the reindeer.

"You have to be quiet tonight.

You mustn't wake the children!"

"I'll try not to," said Santa. "But I *do* like singing!"

Over the moonlit world they sped,
towards the sleeping children.

Santa was so excited that he forgot
to land on the roof of the first house.

"BUSY,
 BUSY,
 BUSY BEE!" roared Santa, coming down
to land in the garden, and meeting a friendly cat.
"Happy Christmas, Cat!"
The cat waved her tail in the air.
"SHHH, SANTA," she whispered back.
"You mustn't wake the children!"
        "Of course I won't," said Santa,
            jumping out of the sleigh.

All the house was sleeping,
as Santa threw the sack over his
shoulder and tiptoed along the
garden path towards the back door.
Only the snowman was awake.

"OOH,
 OOH,
 OOH-OOPS!" cried Santa,
sliding on a patch of ice and crashing
to the ground.

"SHHH, SANTA," whispered the snowman.
"You mustn't wake the children!"
"Sorry," said Santa, picking himself up
and bouncing indoors. "But Christmas *is*
my favourite time of year!"

When he reached the Christmas tree
Santa stopped bouncing, and pulled
some presents from his sack.

A jack-in-the-box burst open,
and made Santa jump in surprise.

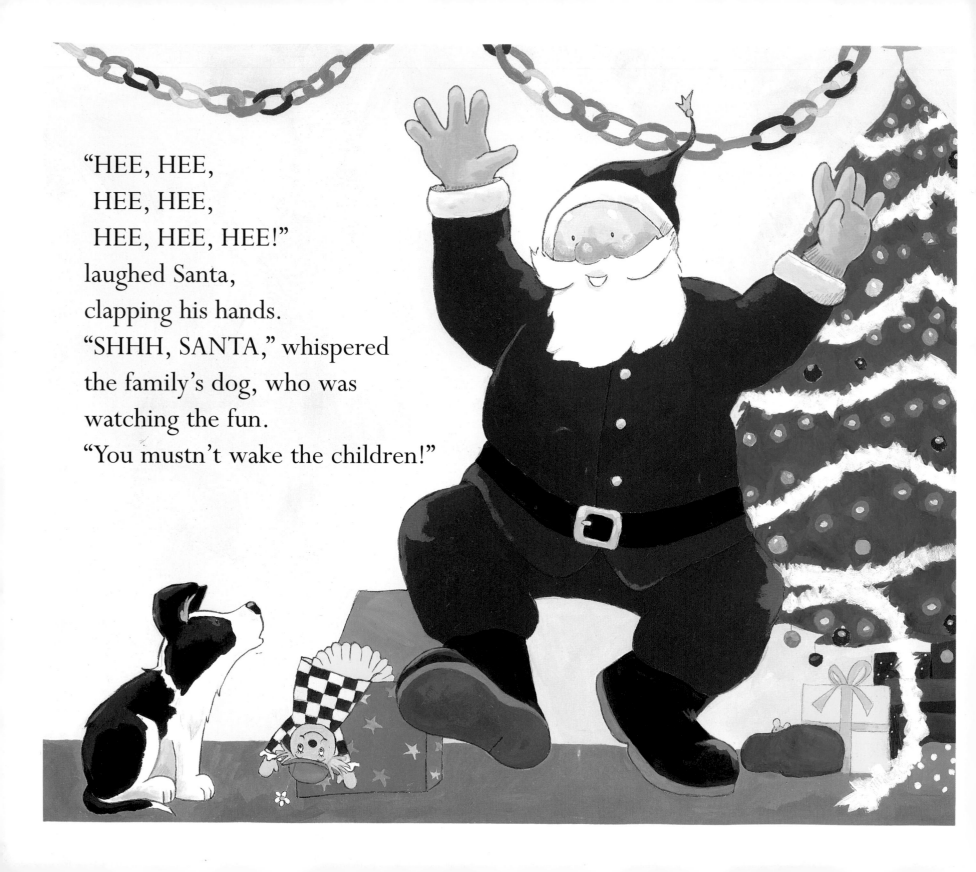

"HEE, HEE,
 HEE, HEE,
 HEE, HEE, HEE!"
laughed Santa,
clapping his hands.
"SHHH, SANTA," whispered
the family's dog, who was
watching the fun.
"You mustn't wake the children!"

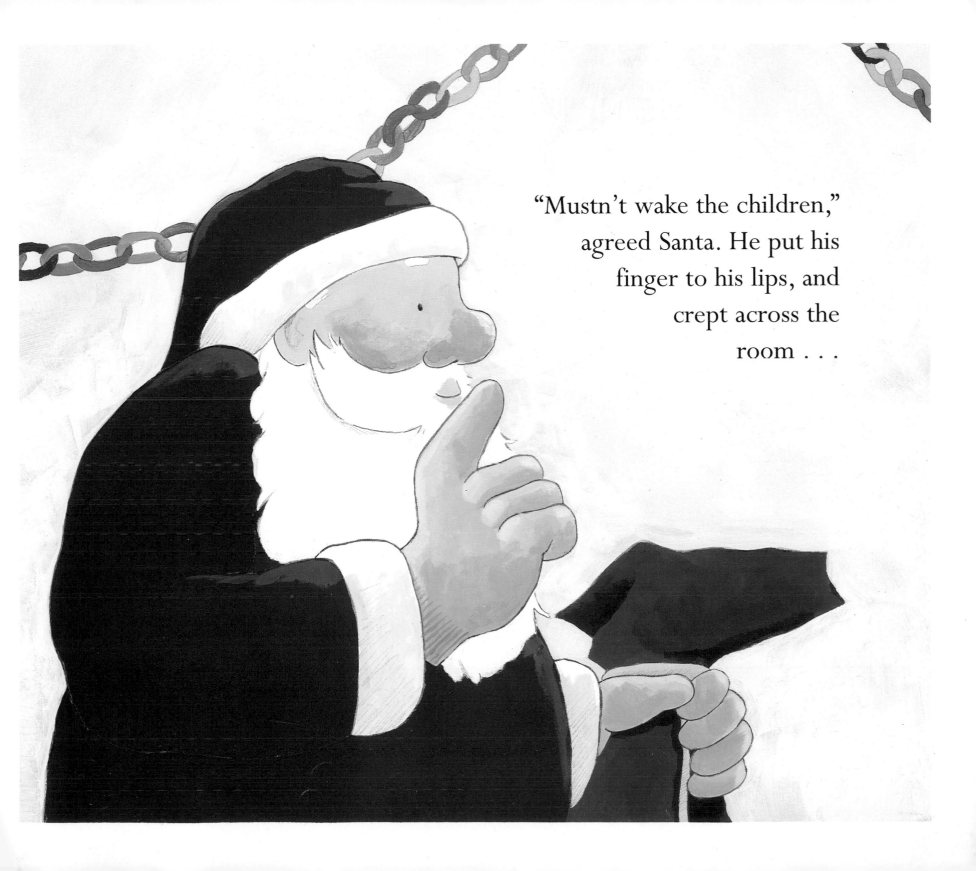

"Mustn't wake the children," agreed Santa. He put his finger to his lips, and crept across the room . . .

. . . but he didn't notice the
tinsel, trailing all over the floor —
until it was too late.
"BUMPITY,
  BUMPITY,
  BUMP!" boomed Santa,
landing on a roller skate.
He skidded across the carpet,
and fell headfirst into the fireplace.
It was a good job the fire was out!

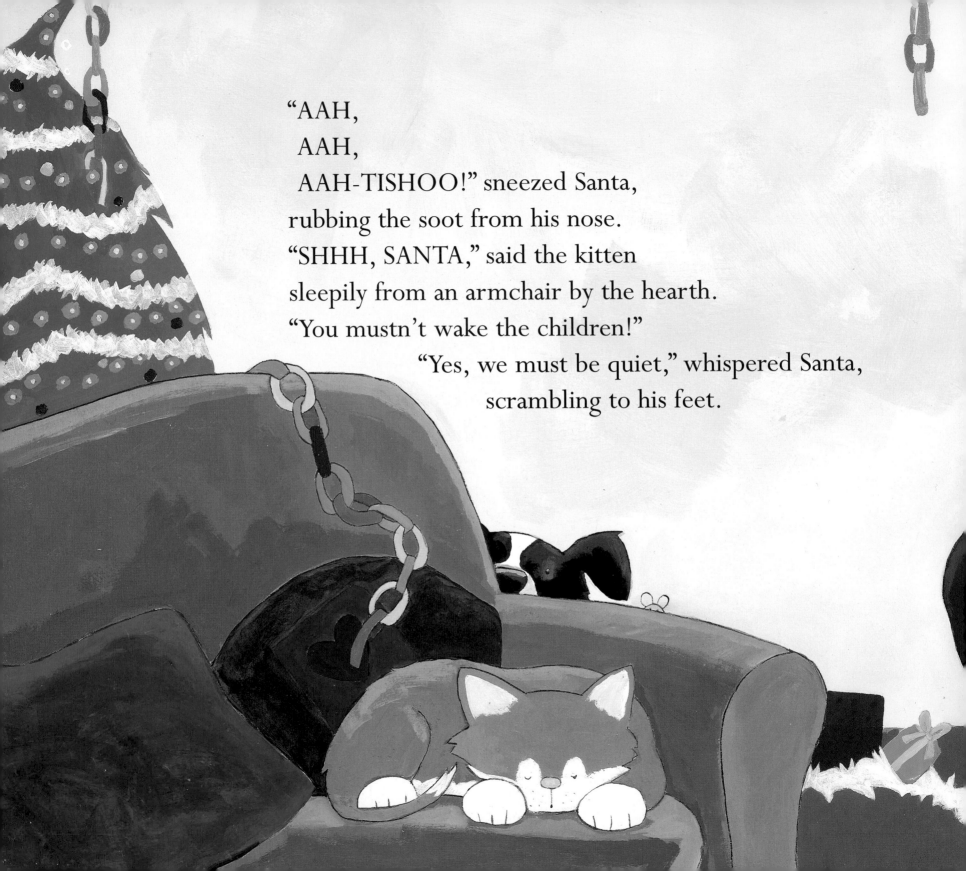

"AAH,
 AAH,
 AAH-TISHOO!" sneezed Santa,
rubbing the soot from his nose.
"SHHH, SANTA," said the kitten
sleepily from an armchair by the hearth.
"You mustn't wake the children!"
          "Yes, we must be quiet," whispered Santa,
                    scrambling to his feet.

Santa picked up his sack and hurried back to his sleigh. There were lots more visits to make before Christmas Day, but at last his sack was empty.

Santa rubbed his eyes sleepily and called,
"Home, Reindeer!"
And with a toss of their heads and a jingle of bells,
the reindeer leapt into the sky.

"HO, HO, HO!" shouted Santa loudly.
"Here we are, home at last!"
"SHHH, SANTA," he added quietly to himself.
"I know, I mustn't wake the children!"

It had been a busy night,
and Santa felt very tired.
He made himself a cup of hot cocoa,
put on his slippers, lay back in his armchair
and fell fast asleep . . .

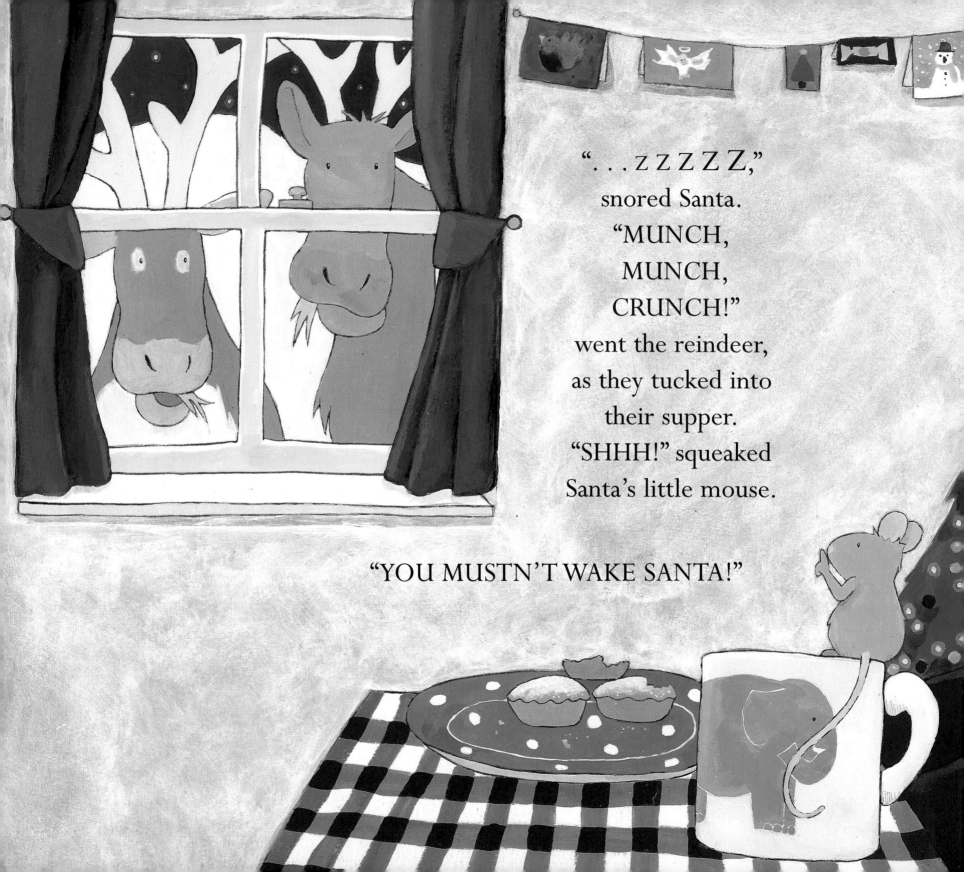

"...ZZZZZ,"
snored Santa.
"MUNCH,
MUNCH,
CRUNCH!"
went the reindeer,
as they tucked into
their supper.
"SHHH!" squeaked
Santa's little mouse.

"YOU MUSTN'T WAKE SANTA!"